PROMISED
TO THE
NIGHT

K. LORAINE

USA Today BESTSELLING AUTHORS

MEG ANNE

For Catherine and Hannah,
It might be a gherkin...but it'll always be a big pickle to us.

Pleasure is sweetest when 'tis paid for by another's pain.

— OVID

PROMISED
TO THE
NIGHT

Authors' Note

Promised to the Night contains mature and graphic content that is not suitable for all audiences. Such content includes dubious consent, degradation, impact and blood play, bondage, and more. **Reader discretion is advised.**

A detailed list of content and trigger warnings is available on our website.

CHAPTER
ONE
ROSIE

"Take me." My words rang out in the council chamber, echoing harsh and strident off the stone walls.

My father took a step forward, protest etched in every line of his body, but before he could utter a word, the High Chancellor held up a hand. "Do you know what you're volunteering for, lass?"

I knew any hint of weakness would be my undoing. Though my knees were practically knocking together, I held my chin high, my voice shockingly steady. It was my life or one of my brothers. I couldn't let them stand in harm's way. If one of us had to die, it may as well be the weak link in our family tree. "I do."

"We don't want her head. We want Noah Blackthorne's," Felicity Donoghue, Duchess of Canterbury, stared down her nose at me as though I was nothing more than a speck of dirt on her frock.

The High Chancellor raised a brow. "One child is much like any other. Why does it matter which Blackthorne pays the blood price, so long as it is paid?"

Gavin Donoghue's gaze found mine from across the room. His expression, intense and brooding, had haunted my dreams more often than I cared to admit. Handsome devil that he was, I wouldn't be surprised to learn those eyes of his could burn through every stitch I was wearing if he wanted them to. I hadn't been this close to him since Noah and Callista signed their betrothal agreement several years ago, but my reaction to his presence was every bit as intense now as it had been then. A flutter took up residence in my belly as arousal built between my thighs and heat burned in my cheeks.

Gavin's eyes widened just a touch, nostrils flaring, and I knew . . . *he* knew what he did to me. The slight quirk of his lips told me he liked it.

And just like that, a dark and tempting thought sparked to life. I couldn't be so bold . . . could I?

It's that or your life, Roslyn. If ever there was a time to be brave.

I wet my lips, clearing my throat before I spoke again. "Lord High Chancellor, might I make a suggestion?"

Once again, every eye in the room landed on me.

"Speak, child. We're listening."

"It was an alliance between the Donoghues and the Blackthornes that was originally sought. It's not too late for such ties to be made."

"Our daughter is dead," Lady Canterbury snarled.

"But I'm not." It took everything in me not to look back at Gavin.

"Rosie, what are you doing? Have you gone mad?" my brother Westley asked in a low voice, shock giving it a panicked quality.

"You?" The Duchess laughed, a high-pitched trill that

2

sent skitters down my spine. "You think you're remotely fit to become a duchess? To wed our son?"

I couldn't respond. She'd hit the target in one well-aimed shot. For all intents and purposes, I was human, like my mother. Although I was the daughter of a vampire king, I'd never turn. That made me weaker than all the rest. Sullied by her blood. Dirty, according to some in the vampire world. If I'd turned before reaching adulthood, things would've been different. They could've overlooked my mother's humanity as they did for both Noah and West. Once the vampire took over, all traces of human DNA were replaced by the dominant genes. It happened from time to time that a child born of a human and vampire union didn't turn. I was one such creature.

My father's hand was a steady weight on my shoulder, reminding me I had their support no matter what. Say what you will about vampires—the Blackthornes took care of their own.

"Mother," Gavin said, his voice rich and mesmerizing. "Hear her out."

"What? You're actually entertaining this ridiculous notion?"

"She has the blood of the sun."

The way her eyes sparkled at his reminder of exactly what I could offer them made my skin crawl. But I knew this was my main bargaining chip. The same blood that damned me to a human life was their saving grace. Pure and unspoiled by being turned, it was magic. Literally. One taste would allow any vampire to walk in the sunlight for an entire day. A deep feeding might provide a week or more of immunity to the light. It was exactly the reason my father had taken my mother all those years ago.

Lady Canterbury's lips turned up in a wicked smile. "So

she does." She strode across the room and reached for me. I clung to my will and forced myself not to flinch away as her icy finger trailed my jaw and down the column of my throat. "Perhaps you're not so useless after all, child."

West vibrated with fury at my side. "Don't you dare speak of my sister that way. She holds more value in her little finger than you do in your entire body."

"Exactly my point, West. Thank you for backing me up. A marriage between Roslyn and I is perhaps more beneficial than one between Noah and Callista. Any child she bears me would prove a stronger bloodline because of her humanity." Gavin's irises were trained on me, hunger banked in their depths. "What you see as weakness, Mother, I see as opportunity."

I shouldn't be so turned on by his casual talk about using me as a broodmare, but dash it all, I was. No one had ever looked at me with the searing intensity I found in Gavin's dark gaze. I felt alive in a way I never had before. It was heady. Addictive. I wanted every unspoken promise reflected in his eyes. Even if I didn't know exactly what I was asking for.

Bloody hell, my knickers were going to be ruined at this rate.

The beautiful bastard smirked, flashing me a hint of fang.

"Are you certain this is what you want, lass? It cannae be undone." The High Chancellor looked me squarely in the eye, and the concern flickering within his features had my belly clenching.

I knew what he was telling me. His thoughts telegraphed as easily as if he said the words aloud even without the benefit of the mind reading abilities my family shared . . . all except me, of course. The Donoghues were vile, wicked creatures. Selfish and hateful. Nothing about them was redeemable, and I was a lamb willingly venturing into their den.

But I wouldn't let my brothers die if I could save them with the simple act of marriage. Especially when the thought of being Gavin's wife was doing such lovely things to my insides. Not all monsters were necessarily the things lurking in our nightmares. Some could be tamed.

Perhaps I'd be the one to tame Gavin Donoghue.

She was the most perfect creature I'd ever seen, and I couldn't wait to destroy her. My cock was a length of steel in my trousers. I could already picture her painted in pain and pleasure, her skin my canvas, her cries my symphony. I was desperate to know what she'd look like with tears trembling on those thick lashes, cheeks flushed, lips parted on a moan. My cum streaked across her thighs, a complement to the pink welts she'd beg me to leave on her skin.

I've never wanted to own anything so badly as I did the woman standing across from me.

Roslyn Blackthorne would be my masterpiece. My toy. My Duchess.

Mine to break and put back together.

Mine to keep.

Mine.

I itched to reach out and take her by the wrist, lead her straight to hell right here and now, but I had to show restraint. Now was not the time. I'd have her soon enough. These things needed to be done a certain way. There were customs to observe. After all, she wasn't simply going to be my submissive. She would be my wife. A different thing altogether.

My father's fingers brushed the top of my hand like the wings of a butterfly. If it weren't necessary, he wouldn't even have done that much. But touch was required to allow his voice to run through my head.

"Are you really willing to tie yourself to this creature for all of her life? She may have the blood of the sun, but she's—"

"Think of the benefits of this, Father. She will bring us more power than we've ever had. We can overthrow the Blackthornes. Unseat them. Take what we want."

"A marriage in name only, then? You'll get her with child and then lock her away?"

I would lock her away, yes, but not in the same sense my father was thinking. He didn't need to know exactly how depraved his son was, though, so I simply agreed.

"Exactly."

His lips lifted, approval shimmering along our mental bond. Perhaps I wasn't the most depraved among us after all. Disgust curled my lip, and I shrugged off the light brush of his fingers. I couldn't stand being touched, least of all by him. Not when every memory of the Duke's attention ended in my pain.

It didn't take a licensed therapist to diagnose the reason for my predilections. My need for control. To administer pain but never receive it. To find pleasure once when my dominance was absolute. I was very aware I had daddy issues.

"Your highness, Lord Donoghue, do you both enter into this betrothal of your own free will?" the High Chancellor asked. It didn't escape me that he made a point of using our antiquated titles. No one called me Lord anything anymore, and the Blackthornes, though they may be royalty, never required their honorifics be used.

Roslyn came toward me, her gaze downcast, head bowed slightly. God, but the things it did to my cock to see her like that. But then she stumbled, falling to her hands and knees on the cool stone floor.

"Rosie!" her brother called, stepping forward to assist her.

"I've got her," I murmured, reaching down to tip her chin up. "Are you all right?"

Her breath hitched, her pupils flaring as she met my gaze. "Y-yes, my lord."

Oh yes. I liked that very much.

Keeping hold of her chin, I brushed the pad of my thumb over her plump lower lip. "So what do you think, petal? Do you really want me as your husband?"

"Yes," she whispered, then more firmly, "I do."

Seeing her there, on her knees, all but begging to be mine, was delicious. Sinful. If we weren't surrounded by both our families, my cock would already be halfway down her throat.

"Very well, I accept." I helped her to her feet, turning over her hand so I could inspect her palm. A bruise was already forming on the delicate skin, and there, just on the edge of her wrist, was a red scrape, blood welling on the surface.

Bringing the mark to my lips, I kissed the place she bled for me and allowed myself a taste of her. Oh, I would have more of this. More of her. Once we were married, there would be no part of this woman I wouldn't own.

Yes, Gavin. Take me. Make me yours. Her voice echoed in my mind, soft and distant but still there. Shocking the hell out of me.

But that hunger for her submission was stronger than anything else, and I flicked my tongue over her wrist one final time as I said the only thing I could.

"Mine."

≈

TOMORROW I WOULD FINALLY HAVE Roslyn in my grasp. Tonight was a celebration. A way to prepare myself for the big day. My stag night, if you will. I wondered if my bride-to-be was having a hen do of her own. But then again, she didn't know the details of all we had in store for her. Poor lamb. I'd show her.

"Donoghue, it's been ages since last we saw your face here." A man I didn't recognize had the nerve to clap me on the shoulder.

"And you are?"

He stared at me, affronted. "Henri. Don't you remember? We met in Paris at my club. You sampled one of my . . . rooms."

"Ah, yes, the incubus."

The Frenchman smirked. "I imagine you must've been pleased with your service at my establishment, yet you've not returned." As an incubus, he knew exactly how much I'd enjoyed myself, no imagination required. The annoying prick.

"*Iniquity* is my club of choice these days."

"Ah yes, Lilith's little den of sin. She is a skilled Mistress, is she not?"

"I wouldn't know."

His violet eyes glimmered. "Oh right, you prefer male companions if I recall correctly."

"The companion is interchangeable so long as I am the Master."

The incubus took a deep breath, clearly feeding off whatever sexual energy I was exuding.

"Did someone say my name? I do so love the sound of men begging for my attention." Lilith Duval slipped her arm around Henri's shoulders. "Hello, darlings. Poaching my clients again, Henri?"

"C'est moi? What cause have I ever given you to think I would do such a thing?"

She raised one perfect brow. "Do you really want me to answer that?"

"He was mine first."

"I am no one's. In case the two of you are operating on the mistaken belief I belong to either of you."

Lilith pressed her crimson lips to my cheek. "A girl can dream. Tell me, Gavin, when can we look forward to your next performance? My patrons did so love your skill with the whip."

The thought of tying Roslyn up in one of *Iniquity's* dark rooms and putting on a show had me rock hard and aching. "Perhaps sooner than you think, Lily dear."

"Lilith." She huffed, then turned her attention toward the ring in the center of the space. "Oh, look. The Mercers are ready to begin."

A pair of shifter twins stepped into the ring, ready to fight. They were mirror images—tall, broad, rugged, and built to defend their territory.

"I do love to watch them work," Lilith purred as one of them removed his shirt. "Don't they just . . . turn you on?" She sucked in a breath, her excitement palpable. "Do you think they do *everything* together?"

I didn't answer, but my gaze was focused on the twins

as a hulking troll stomped through the crowd. The men tensed, ready to take the beast down.

"Oh, Donoghue, I can feel the hunger coming off you in waves. Do you want to come back to the club? Have another go with one of my girls . . . or gentlemen, if that is more to your desire tonight?"

"Or I could just take care of you right here," Henri offered, moving in close.

The temptation to take them up on their offers was strong, but a loud cheer from the crowd pulled all three of us from the lust haze they'd woven around me. The Mercers had taken down the troll in minutes. From the sound of things, a great deal of money was won by some and lost by others.

"So, what will it be, Donoghue? The succubus or moi?"

"Neither, I'm afraid. I'm getting married tomorrow. I require my beauty sleep."

Henri pouted while Lilith grinned. "Fair enough. You know where to find me when you're ready to have a little fun." Her expression brightened, gaze following the two fighters as they walked past. "Oh, Remington, darling! Come over here, love."

Remington, sweat soaked and glistening, joined us, his brother Bentley standing sentry behind him. "Hey, Lil. What's up?"

"Lilith. You know better. Honestly."

A smirk that could only be classified as seductive curled his lips. "Maybe I wanted to be punished."

"Oh, that can be arranged. You know I'm a fan of the bad boys. Perhaps I'll give you to Gavin here. He's very good at delivering pain."

"Touch him, and I'll . . . b–b–break your f–f–fucking

11

hand," his brother growled. Somehow the stammer didn't take away from his ferocity. Interesting.

"Bentley, doll, don't be a spoilsport."

"He's not. He's just protective."

"He needn't worry. I'm not Lilith's to gift."

Remington raked his gaze over my body. "Too bad. I'm always up for a way to blow off extra . . . adrenaline after a match."

I had to admit, he'd look good with my fingerprints marking his skin. But then Roslyn's amber eyes flashed in my mind, and I schooled my thoughts.

"Remi, h–he's a f–f–fucking leech."

The twin's gaze cooled considerably. "Guess it's for the best then. Even I have standards."

My jaw clenched, and I had to swallow back the flurry of insults my honor demanded I hurl their way. These dogs were beneath me. It wasn't worth the energy required to put them in their place.

"I'd say it's been a pleasure, chaps, but I'm no liar. I've more pressing matters that require my attention." I caught the eye of the very man I was set to meet on the outskirts of the crowd. "Remington, Bentley, may we never have to lay eyes on each other again."

"Fuck off, asshole." That time Ben didn't stutter.

Storming away from the group, I made a beeline for the entire reason I was really here. A gift for my bride. Something to ensure she never forgot who owned her.

"Donoghue. Took you long enough. I was about to give up on you." The warlock patted his pocket. "I've got what you asked for. Do you have my payment?"

"Do you doubt my word?" My hands flexed as anticipation raced through me. "The money is already in your account."

He pulled out his phone and made a show of swiping across the screen, clearly checking to make sure I wasn't lying. Once he was satisfied, he handed me a velvet-wrapped package.

It took everything in me not to open it and inspect the gift here and now, but something as valuable as this couldn't be flaunted amongst the rabble in attendance here in the undercroft. Besides, I'd much rather admire my purchase as I made Roslyn mine for the first time.

Smiling, I pocketed the treasure, already eagerly anticipating the taste of my bride's virgin blood.

CHAPTER

THREE

ROSIE

A FEW WEEKS LATER

T'd never left my family for longer than a night or two. Honestly, the prospect of starting a new life, being Gavin's bride . . . it thrilled me in a way nothing else had. I might pretend otherwise, especially around Noah, but Gavin had always been the object of my desires. Even though he rarely, if ever, had shown me any interest.

And why would he? He was nearly a decade my senior, and I was just the annoying little sister of *his* sister's fiancé —now of his sister's murderer. Apprehension curled in my belly. That tidbit was something I hadn't allowed a place in my brain. Noah had done what he must to survive Callista's betrayal, but now we were all paying the price for it.

Gently folding the last piece of clothing I could fit in my luggage, I settled the silk nightgown atop the rest of my belongings.

I'd been so focused on my task that a little scream escaped when a knock came at the door.

"Sorry," my brother grinned, "didn't mean to frighten you. Just wanted to check and see how packing was going."

"Likely story, Westley. You live to terrorize me."

"It's a little brother's job to be a nuisance."

I wrinkled my nose and bent to gather the silk that had slipped from my fingers. "I thought you were supposed to grow out of that."

"Never."

"Your future mate is a lucky . . . person."

One dark brow rose, but he didn't say anything. Instead, West headed into my walk-in closet, disappearing into the depths. When he returned, he held my tattered stuffed octopus in both hands.

"You can't possibly be leaving to face the Donoghues without Mr. Wiggles."

I laughed as he shook the plush toy, making the legs writhe and remind me how the beloved creature acquired his name.

Adopting an outlandish voice, he made the toy speak. "You can't leave me behind, Rosie. I'm your best friend. Who else will protect you from the big bad duke?"

I snatched Mr. Wiggles from West and held him close, comfort settling over me instantly. The thing was, he *had* protected me from nightmares ever since the night my aunt Natalie gave him to me. Pressing my face into the soft pink fabric, I kissed his lumpy head and sighed.

"Sorry, Mr. Wiggles. I can't bring you with me this time. You'll have to keep West safe instead."

Westly accepted my offering, this time making an exaggerated pout. "But I wuv you, Wosie-kins."

"And I you. You've been a most excellent octopus, but I feel West might need you more than I."

"Doubtful," Westley said, employing his true voice once more as he sat down on my bed. "You're walking into a pit of vipers, Roz. For God's sake, you can't even say the word fuck without stumbling over it."

"I can."

The look he gave me called that a lie. "Say it."

"I don't want to."

"See."

"Fork you, West."

He didn't laugh. My brother's eyes were dark with worry. "I can't believe this is what you truly want."

"What I want is for you to stay alive. I can deal with snakes. I'm stronger than you give me credit for. I fought off that fae attack while you were off doing God knows what in Canada."

He puffed out his chest. "It was a diplomatic mission."

"Oh yes, what was his name? Waderick?"

West flushed but chose a new tactic. "Roz, I don't trust them. Minutes before accepting the betrothal, they were screaming for our heads. They can't possibly mean you anything but harm. And we won't even be nearby to protect you."

"Noah spends most of his time in England. He'll be close enough if I need him." I bit the inside of my cheek, knowing that was probably a lie. My older brother currently had his hands full trying to locate his missing mate. Who knew when he'd return to London? If he came back at all.

"They're not above killing any of us. Do you really think they'll be satisfied with your marriage to Gavin? Roz, they're going to chain you up and drain you after they make you their breeding bitch so they can have more of our blood. They're just like Grandfather."

I winced. Our father had killed the king for trying the very same thing with Mother. If he hadn't, none of us would exist.

"Gavin doesn't seem as bad as the rest of them. He came to my rescue when I fell."

"Is that what you're calling it? He also took your blood without your consent. He probably spent the day strolling in the sunlight because of you. Did you think about that? I've heard things about him, Roz. Dark things. He's the worst of the lot."

That made me laugh. West was nearly as sheltered as I; what could he possibly have heard that I hadn't? "Such as?"

"He has . . . dark inclinations."

"Inclinations? West, he's a vampire. He feeds on blood. Of course he's got dark appetites. That comes with the territory."

My brother reached out and grabbed my wrist. "No, you aren't listening. He's sick. Twisted. He can't get off without hurting his partners. He . . ." West huffed out a breath before blurting, "He's a murderer, Roslyn."

"And that's supposed to deter me? Our parents are murderers, our brother too. I challenge you to find a single vampire in our vicinity who hasn't killed at least once." I shot him a pointed look, knowing it was a low blow.

"Roz, you still don't get it. If he could do that, hurt someone he's supposed to care about, what do you think he's going to do to his *wife*? You will have little to no protection from him. He will hurt you. Demean and debase you. You're too good and pure for the likes of him."

If I was so pure, why did a spark of dangerous interest ignite somewhere in the darkest part of me at the mention of Gavin having his way with me? "You don't have a say in this, brother. It's already done." I snapped my suitcase closed to emphasize the point. "I leave in an hour."

"You could run. It's not too late. I'd cover for you. We could call that hacker Noah spoke with. Asher something."

Little did my baby brother know I'd already looked into Asher Henry the second my brother placed his trust in the man. I found every scrap of information that existed about him, which wasn't much, but I bet it was still more than most knew. Asher wasn't the only one skilled at ferreting out secrets.

"I'm not running, West. I chose this."

He deflated a little, looking more boy than man for the first time in years. "I just don't want you to get hurt."

"That's part of living, sweet brother. You can't keep me in a bubble."

"Father would if he could."

"So would Noah."

"Then I'll step aside and let you be free."

He surprised me then, standing and pulling me into his arms. He was still all lanky limbs and wiry muscle, but in a few more years, he'd reach full maturity and stop aging at his peak physical self. I wondered if I'd be around to see it. Something told me becoming a Donoghue meant leaving my Blackthorne side in the past.

I held him tight, a wave of emotion hitting me hard, sending tears to my eyes as I breathed in his scent.

"I'll be fine. I promise."

"If you're not, I swear I will burn them to the ground."

"Of course you will. That is the Blackthorne way."

He clung to me a little tighter. "I'll miss you, Roz."

"I'll miss you too. Try not to worry too much, West. The

Apocalypse is nigh. So if things really do go tits up, at least I won't have to suffer for long."

It was callous to joke about everything my brother and his mate were dealing with, but in the grand scheme of things, wasn't it far worse to be the harbinger of the end times than the wife of a wicked vampire lord?

It had to be . . . right?

CHAPTER
FOUR
ROSIE

"You can do this, Roslyn. It's just a house. They're just vampires. You grew up with vampires. It's nothing to be afraid of."

I stared up at the Donoghue family estate.

Let's call a spade a spade, Rosie. It's a forking castle, for fork's sake.

As I stood there counting the turrets, the door opened, and a pinched-faced woman peered out.

"Well, are ye coming in, or are ye going tae make us wait even longer?"

Her Scottish brogue was harsh and so thick I could barely understand her, aside from the obvious annoyance in her tone.

"Yes, sorry." Tightening my hold on the suitcase in my hand, I rushed up the steps and into the foyer.

"Don't dawdle. We havenae got all night." She stormed through the cavernous hall until she reached the grand staircase.

Ostentatious. That was the only word to describe this . . . home? . . . prison? Which would it be? Blackthorne

Manor was my home. It had been a safe place for the last twenty-one years. Never had it felt cold to me. But this castle filled my bones with a chill so deep they ached.

You know what castles have? Dungeons. Places they keep people they want to punish.

The dark thoughts made me shiver, and I nearly tripped in my haste to get up the stairs. The housekeeper hadn't stopped to make sure I was following, and she was already halfway down the next hall before I caught up with her.

There weren't any carpets on the stone flooring, and the sounds of my footsteps bounced off the walls, emphasizing the noise. It was the only noise.

Frowning, I glanced out the window. It was nearly dark. Where was everybody? My father would already be awake, and a household of this size required significant staff to keep it running smoothly. Something was off.

"Where is everyone?"

The woman huffed. "Enough with yer incessant questions."

This was my first. God, she is prickly.

She reached a door at the end of the hall, just before the first bend that would lead down another maze of rooms. Throwing it open, she gestured inside. "In with ye. There's a dress yer tae wear hanging in the wardrobe. I suggest ye get yerself sorted quickly, or ye'll be coming down in that . . . frock. Thirty minutes. Not a second more."

"What if I'm not ready in thirty minutes?" I could be ready in ten, but that wasn't the point. This lady was—as Noah would say—a right see-you-next-Tuesday.

"Then yer coming down in yer knickers."

Wouldn't that be a statement? Gavin wouldn't have to wonder what I looked like under my clothes.

"I'll make sure they are a matching set then, shall I?"

21

The stare she sent me was indifferent. "I dinnae care what they look like. Now, shift yerself. His lordship doesnae like to be kept waiting."

With that she slammed the door.

"Aren't you a peach?" I muttered, shaking my head as I took in my accommodations. The room was lovely, but as cold as the rest of the house. The four-poster bed had snowy white linens. The large hearth was currently empty, but I could imagine how inviting the room would be with a fire's soft glow.

Spinning in a circle, I spotted the dress they'd left for me. Or should I say gown?

What an odd choice for a family dinner.

"Is that a petticoat?" Moving toward the ivory satin and lace number, I counted the number of fluffy underskirts. "They're blooming mad if they think I'll be able to get this monster on in thirty minutes."

With ten seconds to spare, I secured the final fastenings on the bodice, my breasts nearly spilling out of the top of the gown. I couldn't go down to my future in-laws looking like this. I was still in the middle of trying to shove them back into the fabric when the door opened without so much as a knock.

"Och, you'd think ye've never worn a dress before. Probably havenae, ye Blackthorne beastie." I would've corrected her, but she spun me around, shoved her hands into my dress, and pulled my boobs up until my nipples were all but popping free of the neckline. Then she adjusted the thin straps so they sat draped over my arms, baring my shoulders. "They'll be wanting to see all ye have to offer."

"So it would seem."

"I'll say this for ye. Ye have plenty to display. His lordship will be pleased, if nothing else."

"I thought it was Gavin I needed to be pleasing to."

With a sly look, she nodded. "Aye. It is. But the duke will want his due as well."

She didn't mean what I thought she meant . . . surely she didn't. That would be . . . I shuddered, unable to find the words to express how absolutely revolted I was by the thought of Gavin's father's hands—or fangs—coming anywhere near me.

Fork me.

The miserable woman grabbed my elbow and tugged me out of the room. "Come on, then. They're waiting."

In a whirl of skirts, I followed, her grip not giving me much choice. I had no idea where I was or which way to go to return to my room by the time we reached a pair of polished wood French doors.

The doors swung open without being touched, revealing a room bathed in candlelight. Candelabras lined a makeshift aisle, and four figures stood at the other side in a little group. One of them turned as the doors opened.

"Finally."

I barely registered the duchess's clipped voice. I was too consumed by the sight of Gavin in profile. My breath caught as he turned his stare on me. The most handsome man I'd ever seen. The first one I'd ever responded to in . . . *that* way. He was dressed in black-tie formalwear, the cut of his tuxedo jacket doing amazing things for his shoulders. But it was the way his eyes burned, a deep molten chocolate so dark they were nearly black, that sent my knees wobbling. Not to be outdone, my knickers dampened in response as well.

"Now that the bride has seen fit to grace us with her presence, shall we get this over and done with?" The duchess offered me an impatient look as she stepped aside to reveal an altar, complete with a silver ceremonial spike I knew all too well.

Oh, fork.

I wasn't here to plan the wedding. This *was* the wedding.

FIVE

I should have felt bad my little princess didn't know what she'd truly been brought here for. But I didn't. The Blackthornes had proven time and again they couldn't be trusted. This was the only way to ensure the marriage came to pass.

I would not be denied. I would not be made a fool.

The shock on Roslyn's face sent a jolt of arousal coursing through me, fueling my need to chase her and assert my dominance.

"I . . . what's going on?" Bloody hell, I loved the fear in her voice. The way her pulse spiked as understanding settled in even as she asked the question.

"Come to me, princess. Let's finish this so we can get to the fun part."

I held out my hand for her, and a strange tremor had me fighting for control as I waited.

Her fingers fisted in her skirt, but she didn't move.

Anger burned through the arousal.

"Do not make me come over there, petal. Because when I reach you, I will shove you down and make you crawl for wasting my time. I do not think you want to debase yourself like that in front of my parents, but that's exactly what will happen because I will not let you rise until this ceremony is completed. We're getting married tonight. It's your choice to do it standing on your own two feet at my side or on your knees before me."

Her little intake of breath said it all. I'd won, and she liked it. "Yes, my lord."

Oh, how fucking perfect.

With each step she took, threads of my control broke. I wanted this over with already, wanted her in my room, submitting to my commands, giving herself over to me. I needed to take her and make her mine in every way.

The ceremony was a blur, a simple formality as we agreed to the words uttered by the council representative. Then we reached the pivotal moment, the joining.

"Hold out your hands," the councilman said.

I laid mine out first, palm up, and waited for my sweet petal to do the same. She hesitated, her eyes locking on mine.

"Now, petal. Do as you're told."

The moment she did, I knew something was wrong. An electric sensation coursed through me at the contact, a hum of anticipation, like the promise of a wild storm.

The councilman drove the silver spike through the center of our palms, mingling our blood, forging a connection and opening a box inside me I'd thought forever locked.

"Joined by blood and pain, the two of you are one. Heal your bride." He pulled the spike free, and I was left staring at the wound in stunned silence.

But I did my duty. I brought my free wrist to my lips and broke my skin before dripping my blood over her hand. She healed quickly, the hammering of her pulse loud in my ears and synced perfectly with my own heart.

"Henceforth, you shall be known as Roslyn Donoghue. Your former name no longer exists. My deepest felicitations to you, the future Duchess of Canterbury."

Roslyn had barely made a sound during the ceremony. She blinked slowly at the title, her eyes locked on me when they opened as if asking what came next.

There was one final thing I needed to do before this was over. Cock hard as steel, I took a deep breath, already scenting her body's reaction to me. Gripping her by the nape of her perfect neck, I pulled her hard against me and bared my fangs. Then I struck, feeding on her, making her whimper, and rocking my hips into her as I did.

"Gavin," she whispered on a soft moan.

One word flashed through my mind like a bolt of lightning illuminating the night as it all came together. Her heart beating in time with mine. My intense need for her. The sense of absolute rightness between us as I fed.

Mate.

Oh, fuck.

This changes everything.

How could she be my fated mate? I didn't have one. The Seer had said as much when my parents took both my sister and me to her when we came of age. It was the entire reason Callista had been promised to Noah Blackthorne. Well, the reason the Blackthornes ultimately agreed to the match. The alliance had always been a bigger boon for our family than theirs. But no one could argue with fate.

I wiped my bride's blood off my lips and stepped back from her still trembling form. Every instinct inside me said to protect, provide for, and cherish this delicate creature. Every one but the darkest. That part of me wanted to see her marked and covered in my spend. Even now, the trail of blood dripping into her dress begged for me to smear it across her skin so I could spend hours licking her clean.

How could I hurt the one person I was supposed to safeguard?

The dual urges would be my undoing.

Not stopping to think about what I was doing, I scooped Roslyn into my arms.

28

"Gavin, where are you going? The banquet—"

"To hell with the banquet."

"He needs to consummate the marriage, Felicity. That way there can be no doubt by the Blackthornes that the deed is done." My father's voice was filled with knowing pride.

"Very well, but come join us when you're done. It's rude to ignore your guests."

I didn't answer her. Roslyn snuggled against me, trusting and innocent and all mine. My father was right about one thing. I had to consummate this union. The thought of seeing her virgin's blood streaked down the length of my cock sent a shiver through me.

I swept through the castle, single-minded in my focus. I was nearly shaking with my need to sink inside her by the time we reached her door. With my hands full of her, I couldn't reach the doorknob, and I had half a mind to kick the damned thing in when her sweet voice stopped me.

"No one's ever bitten me before," she whispered. "It . . . made me feel things."

"What sorts of things?"

I set her on her feet and pressed her into the solid wall next to her door. The way she bared her throat to me had my cock kicking against my trousers. But I couldn't take her right here.

"Between my thighs. A tingle. A heavy ache."

Good God.

"Shall I do it again?"

Why was I asking? I never asked. I took.

"Yes."

Dipping my head, I traced the bite mark I'd left with my tongue, and she shuddered, the sound of my name a ragged gasp as it left her lips.

I'd never wanted a woman's moans the way I wanted hers. Her pain? Absolutely. But her sighs of pleasure? Those disarmed me.

I sank my fangs into her tender flesh, my fingers gathering her skirt and pulling it up. I needed to touch her, feel how wet she was for me. I had to know if I did the same things to her as she did to me. One finger parted her folds, and I found her slick and hot.

Fuck.

"I thought it would hurt. The biting," she moaned, arching into me and raking her fingers through my hair, pressing me against her.

"It doesn't?" I breathed the words against her skin as I sank my finger deep inside.

"N-no."

"What does it feel like?"

"Like . . . " She licked her lips, rocking forward onto my hand. "Like you aren't drawing from my neck but from . . . down there."

The fact that my body was so primed and I hadn't even inflicted an ounce of pain sent me spiraling. I couldn't think of a time that had ever happened.

Yet another tick in the mate box.

"Would you like me to draw from . . . down there, petal?" I worked her slowly, the heel of my palm grazing her swollen little clit.

A spark of apprehension flickered in her gaze. "Is that something you want?"

"I want to make you feel good." I said the words without thinking, surprising myself enough to make me falter as I fucked her with my finger.

"Yes. I want you to draw from me everywhere, Gavin. Use me however you want. I'm yours, my lord."

My lord. Christ, those words falling from her lips. My cock was weeping for her.

I sank a second finger in. She was so tight I was sure she would cry out, but all she did was grind down on me, welcoming the invasion.

"Gavin?" A slight hint of panic was laced in that one cry of my name.

"Yes, petal? Tell me what you need."

"Something . . . oh God, something is happening."

Heat swept through me at the realization. "Have you never touched yourself, petal?" My balls drew tight in anticipation of what was about to happen. What *I* was about to give her.

"No. Not like this. It's never felt like this when I—"

"When you come. Say it."

She let out a soft whimper as I curled my fingers. "When I c–come."

My groan was a ragged thing against her ear. "Oh, yes. Even if my fingers weren't buried inside you, I could smell how wet you are for me. Come for me, wife. Show me just how tight this cunt can grip me. Show me how you'll milk my cock."

"Gavin," she cried. And a flood of wetness coated my fingers as she did exactly as I commanded.

I pulled my fingers free of her and brought them to my lips, sucking them clean of her slick honey.

Blinding pleasure raced through me in response, my knees buckling as release hit me with no warning. I had to brace myself against the wall with my free hand to keep from falling as I came in my pants like an untried youth.

I went utterly still, the shock of my orgasm breaking through the pleasure-filled fog she'd wrapped me in. She continued to pant, but when she opened her eyes and stared up at me with absolute devotion, panic clawed its way up my throat.

She reached up and ran her fingertips between my brows. "I knew I would enjoy being your wife."

What had she done to me? I was not this man. I didn't even *know* this man.

I pulled away from her, needing space, time to deal with the crisis her presence created within me. It felt as if I was at war with myself. One side begged me to take her to bed and finish what we started. The other wanted to punish her for making me act like something I wasn't.

I couldn't offer her sweetness or romance. She shouldn't expect it from me. I had no love to give.

Shutting down, I rebuilt the walls she'd taken a wrecking ball to in one night. "Go to your room. I'm done with you."

Her face fell, and she stopped looking at me with those dangerous emotions flickering behind her eyes. Now I saw the expression I'd grow accustomed to. One of hurt. Eventually it would be apathy. She'd distance herself and learn to keep her unwanted feelings to herself. Then I could go back to what I needed without guilt eating away at me.

"Good night, my lord."

Anxiety boiled, rising in my chest to constrict around my heart. I had to reclaim the man I was. I had to control myself, my needs. I had to prove that she hadn't changed me with a single taste.

I was still the demon I knew myself to be. The one who desired above everything else to inflict pain. I'd earned my name long ago, and I would not have the title stripped from me by a pretty virgin with a cunt that tasted like sugar. I simply needed to remind myself exactly who I was.

The Duke of Tears.

I forced my legs to hold me up as I watched him walk away, his posture tense while I was still mostly bone-less, aftershocks of my release skittering over my body like small bursts of lightning.

What did I do wrong?

Biting my lip, I thought back to the whirlwind of the last hour. For a moment it felt as if we'd been completely in sync. Two souls straining toward each other, attempting to become one. I'd even thought . . . perhaps that was simply the dream of a hopeless romantic—a fool. There was no way Gavin Donoghue was my mate.

His actions proved it.

I'd imagined it all.

I'd wanted it all too much.

I'd seen my parents, brother, and uncle all find their fated mates. How much more rose colored could my glasses have been? True mate bonds weren't commonplace. The likelihood I'd find mine here with this man was slim to none. Just because everyone around me found their soulmate didn't mean I would. In fact, the odds were against me.

Three out of four pairs in the supernatural world weren't destined matches. So why would I think I'd be so lucky?

The way he shut me out after stealing my pleasure still burned in my mind as I stared down the empty hall. I still couldn't figure it out. He'd urged me on, pushing me over the edge into sweet oblivion, and then seemed almost angry about it. He hadn't even found his own release. Had he?

I may not have much—any—experience in the sex department, but I knew where things were supposed to go. Insert tab A into slot B and wiggle it around. His tab hadn't gone anywhere near my slot. But those fingers did.

I shivered at the memory, another jolt running through me.

God, those fingers. Who forking knew? I'd touched myself. Obviously. I'd have to be dead not to have urges, but I'd never found that little spot he'd pressed inside me. The one that turned me hot and cold and shut down all autonomous thought. He'd owned me body and soul in that moment. He had absolute control over me. I'd have given him anything he wanted. Everything.

But instead he left.

Finally gathering myself enough to stand without the support of the wall, I opened the bedroom door and stumbled inside, my pleasure bleeding into shame. I was so undesirable my own husband couldn't bring himself to take me.

The heavy gown rustled with each step I took, the sound grating, the thing feeling more like a straight jacket than a dress at this point. I'd hoped Gavin would be the one to remove it in a flurry of need, but now, thinking of our encounter in the hall, perhaps I'd repulsed him instead. I'd been a panting, moaning harlot. Ready to roll over and welcome him inside me, this man I barely knew. Desperate. Bloody shameful.

Weren't virgins supposed to be shy? To act with more dignity?

I wouldn't know. I hadn't got to ask any. It wasn't a topic of conversation amongst my handful of acquaintances at school. People were too scared of the Blackthorne name to get too close to me. And I couldn't exactly ask my husband about the proper way to behave now.

It was times like this I wished I had a sister. I'd been cursed with brothers instead. All the good they did me. Noah was a notorious playboy . . . until he met his match in Sunday. And West . . . well, he might understand men better than I did, but I couldn't discuss this with him. He was too young. He wouldn't know much more than me at eighteen, surely. Right?

I swallowed back a scream of frustration, feeling so bloody stupid. I was smart. *Really* smart. Top of my class. But when it came to anything of actual value, I was a useless ninny. I couldn't be any more of a bluestocking romance heroine if I put on a corset and a Regency frock.

Oh, but Gavin would look dashing with a pair of breeches and one of those puffy shirts, my traitorous thoughts interrupted.

"Stop. It," I growled to myself, pacing back and forth in front of the empty fireplace. "You are a Blackthorne. Get yourself together. You are better than this, Roslyn."

Right. I needed a shower. They always made everything better. I did my best thinking in the isolation of my shower stall. The water rushing over my skin, heating my body, the only sound the spray on tile. No one else to intrude. What-ever my problem, I always felt better after taking one. More in control. More myself. And right now, I desperately needed to feel like anything other than a confused little virgin.

I pulled my wedding dress off, leaving a trail of petti-coats in my wake as I moved to the bathroom and turned on the water.

As I stood beneath the steamy spray, my thoughts raced and my determination grew. He'd wanted me. I'd felt his hardness against my hip, heard his rough voice, thick with desire. Gavin Donoghue wasn't operating under some misguided disgust at my wantonness. Something more had to be going on. Was he worried he'd hurt me when he took my virginity? Did he need me to be more gentle and assure him I was ready?

Maybe the intensity of his feelings had caught him off guard. This was an arranged marriage after all, not a love match. Perhaps he was reeling from the discovery as much as I was?

Did he need reassurance that I wanted him, that he wasn't alone in his need for me?

I could give him that. I'd give him the family he so clearly didn't have. Gavin needed someone to love him. To fix those broken edges that made him so sharp. I could do that for him.

I would.

In fact, I would start doing it right forking now.

I CAUGHT his scent as soon as I stepped into the hall. Leather and ink, the smoky bite of tobacco. Those were things uniquely Gavin. I'd never again set foot in a library and not think of him. Thankfully, my father's bloodline afforded me enhanced senses even though I'd never fully transition into a vampire. I latched on to those distinct aromas and chased the trail my husband had left for me.

I knew I'd reached his room because his scent was saturated here—and fresh. I knocked on the heavy wooden door, fighting the nerves attempting to overtake me.

"Gavin? It's me."

No answer.

Be bold, Roslyn.

Instead of knocking again, I pushed inside. It took less than a second to determine he wasn't there, but a newly discovered rebellious streak had me shutting the door and moving further into my husband's private sanctuary.

So this was where he spent his time. It suited him. Rich woods, plush carpeting, all dark and masculine decor. Gavin's jacket from our wedding lay draped across the bed, and on instinct, I picked it up and brought the fabric to my nose. My nipples pebbled at the memory of him so close, whispering dirty promises in my ear, his teeth on my neck.

"What do you think you're doing, you filthy little thing?" His voice was a harsh rasp across my skin, making me gasp in surprise and drop the coat. I whirled around, an apology already on my lips, but I was alone.

My brows knit in confusion until Gavin's voice sounded again.

"Did I tell you you could touch yourself?"

This time, I realized it came from the laptop he'd left open on his desk.

"I'm sorry, Master. I ache for you. Please. Touch me. I . . . I need you."

"Silence!" The crack of a whip accompanied the barked

command. "You do not have permission to speak unless it is to use your safe word. You know the rules."

I moved closer to the screen, absolutely transfixed by the sight before me. Gavin and another man faced away from the camera, both of them nude.

He trailed the end of his whip along the other man's bloody back. "Unless you are actively seeking punishment. And you know how *disappointed* that sort of behavior makes me. Do you want to disappoint me?"

"No, Master. I'll be good."

The man Gavin had at his disposal turned his body slightly toward the camera, just enough that I could see his swollen erection, the tip glistening as he trembled. The muscles in his arms strained as he clung to the bed's four-poster frame.

"Do you want more?"

The man whimpered something that sounded a bit like he said yes. The lash of the whip cracked so fast I barely registered Gavin had struck, but I felt it right along with his toy. Not on my back, but between my legs. A flood of arousal had me sitting gracelessly in the chair, eyes glued to the computer.

"More," I whispered. "Definitely more."

Gavin strolled leisurely around the unnamed man, giving me a better view of his beautiful, strong body. There was no denying my husband was a veritable Greek god. He looked as if he'd been sculpted by God himself. There wasn't an unattractive bone in his body. From his tousled hair and firm jaw to the flex of his muscles as he moved, every inch was perfection. And my eyes were currently trained on the oh-so-perfect inches between his legs.

That was meant to fit inside me? How?

Thick and veiny . . . I'd never wanted to touch something more. With my mouth. My tongue. Whatever he'd let me get away with.

My fingers trailed down my chest and then along my inner thighs until I reached the soft cotton of my knickers. Curling my fingers under the band, I tugged them down and kicked them off so I could explore myself freely. Then, still watching Gavin, I found that magic little button he'd ground against in the hallway. His jaw flexed, his left hand now wrapped around the base of his . . . *himself*. I licked my lips and imagined I was the object of his desire.

It didn't even occur to me to be jealous. I was too turned on.

"Gavin," I rasped as he stroked his arousal, his eyes closed and head thrown back.

The man at his mercy gave a shuddering moan, and ropes of white spilled onto the black silk sheets on the bed. He hadn't been touched. How on earth had he . . . arrived so easily?

Gavin's hand went still, and he glanced back.

"And now you've made a mess of my sheets. That orgasm was mine, and you stole it from me. Clean up your mess—no, with your tongue. I'll deal with you shortly."

My skin was hot and cold all at the same time, the angry red in Gavin's cheeks only adding fuel to my fire. I wanted him to be cross with me for stealing my own pleasure, to use that deep, dominant voice on me. I needed him to make me his and claim my submission. Why hadn't he brought me to this room if this was the true Gavin Donoghue?

My desire cooling as those thoughts intruded, I moved to stop touching myself, but Gavin's form filled the screen, his face, chest, and hips in full view. That furrow between his brows grew deeper as he spit into his palm, then gripped his manhood firmly once more and began a slow stroke.

Oh, my.

I should have stopped watching. Who was I kidding? I should never have started watching. But now I was a helpless slave to my desire for him. I needed to be part of his pleasure, even if it was stolen.

He'd made me come apart at his hand, and now I wanted to know what it looked like when he did the same to himself. Even if I wasn't the cause. Maybe I could learn him. I had always been a quick study.

Without realizing it, I'd timed my breaths with his. My fingers circled my aching flesh at the same speed he worked his hand over himself. His eyes pinched tightly closed, and he almost appeared in pain as his jaw ticked and a flush crept up his neck.

"Gavin, yes, please make me—" My words cut off as he grunted, his right arm shooting forward, muscles flexing, abs tensing as he found his release.

I cried out as I fell apart with him, my legs shaking as that liquid rush swept through me. It was nowhere near what he'd done to me in the hall, but I couldn't have stopped myself from falling over the edge with him if I'd tried. Even through a screen, Gavin owned my pleasure.

Taking a deep breath, he reached for something out of the camera's sight. He returned with a towel, then wiped away the evidence of his orgasm.

"I could have helped you with that, Master."

"That's not what you're here for. Now turn around and prepare to take your punishment for being an insolent pet."

The other man braced himself, and even through the echoing tingles of my climax, I found myself doing the same. Before now, I'd never craved the bite of a whip, but watching the masterful way Gavin moved turned what should have been horrific and degrading into something beautiful. Like a ballet or an opera. Even the man's cries were a vital piece of the performance.

I wanted to be part of it.

I wanted to know what it felt like to be fully lost to the moment.

A slave to my pleasure and the needs of my body.

To be his.

And when Gavin finally gave his pet permission to finish and helped him lie down, then cared for the wounds gracing his back by healing them with his blood, I wanted that too.

The tenderness.

The devotion.

His love.

"You little fool," I breathed. "This is not your world. Gavin knows it. You'll never be enough to make him truly happy."

I'd gotten so swept up by what the men were doing that I hadn't realized Gavin was no longer on the screen. Heart in my throat, I righted my skirt and fled his room, certain of two things.

I was in love with the idea of my husband, and he would never love me.

EIGHT

GAVIN

I couldn't force Roslyn from my mind no matter how bloody hard I tried. Even in the shower, as I scrubbed my skin raw, thoughts of her assaulted me. The scent of her cunt on my fingers, the taste of her on my tongue, had driven me mad. No one had ever consumed me like this.

Even after finding release, I was still on edge because it hadn't been enough. Simply a pale imitation of what I truly wanted.

But what was worse, the salt in the wound, was my session with Daniel. He deserved more than what he got tonight. He'd been loyal to me for years and allowed us to share something we both needed without the complication of romantic entanglement. Tonight I couldn't even do him the honor of being fully present in the scene with him. All my thoughts were of *her*. It was her body I marked. Hers I claimed. And when I fucked my fist, all I saw was the way she fell apart under my fingers.

Fuck.

My goddamned cock swelled under the towel I'd

wrapped around my hips. She was a problem I needed to solve. But how? I couldn't possibly introduce her to this life. Not when my instinct to bond with her, to ensure she could never leave me, to protect her with every cell in my body, screamed at me and my penchant for pain reared its head. I couldn't have both. She was too innocent to mark, but if I bonded with her, there was no way I'd ever be able to choose another partner to await me on their knees. I'd be as much a slave to her as she would be to me. No one else would suffice, and my honor—I almost laughed at the thought of being honorable—wouldn't allow me to stray from her.

The only reason I was able to fumble my way through the scene with Daniel was that she and I hadn't taken that last step irrevocably tying us to one another. Once a bond was in place, there'd be no one else for me.

Part of me feared that might already be true.

I could still smell her, even now. Her arousal was potent. Sweet. As though she was here, waiting for me.

Excitement and apprehension coiled tight in my gut. Was she here? Had my little bride let herself into my room while I was washing off the evidence of my depravity?

"I smell you, petal. Where are you?"

Fuck. The heady scent of her cunt made my head spin, my length twitching in response. But she was nowhere in the room. Not waiting in my bed. Nor standing at the door. And yet . . . the scent of her was unmistakably present.

She wasn't here now . . . but she had been.

Shit.

My eyes went immediately to the laptop still open on my desk. What had she seen?

But more to the point, what had my little princess *done*?

"You liked it," I whispered.

43

Christ, the things that did to me.

"You want me to pluck you, don't you, petal?"

If she'd let me, I'd take that pretty flower of hers and slowly bruise it until she gave me what I needed. Her complete submission. She'd open for me, blooming beautifully, and eventually I'd be able to do anything . . . *everything*.

A tendril of fear wormed its way into my mind.

Don't you remember what happens to delicate things in your hands? You kill them. You leave them broken. Just like you did with Danika.

I hadn't allowed myself to think of that night in years. I'd lost control. Gone too far, and the person who'd given me their trust paid for their foolishness.

I'd been too young, still learning my own limits and strength. She died because I hadn't been able to stop when it mattered the most.

I could hear her gasps for breath. See the mottled color of her face. But she hadn't used her safe word. She couldn't. Her nails had raked over my cheek, the burn reigniting even at the memory. We'd been so untrained. Not ready for the responsibility of me holding her life in my hands.

In truth, her anguish had driven me on. Watching her suffer triggered my release. I'd been too busy coming to fucking stop.

And so she'd died beneath my hand, unable to breathe as I'd continued to rut like the animal I was.

Rumors were whispered in the dark about Gavin Donoghue and his sinister secret, but being a Donoghue meant my sins never saw the light of day. Everything I'd done had been covered up quickly. Humans disappeared all the time. What was one more missing girl? All my father had needed to do was sign a big enough check, and it all went away.

For them, at least. I still carried the weight of my deeds on my back like a boulder.

I shuddered as Danika's face was replaced by Roslyn's. *The Blackthornes would never be so easily mollified. They'd never stop searching for her.*

A flash of my palm around Roslyn's throat sent a lick of heat through me, but I pushed it aside.

Never. Again.

I hadn't attempted breath play since, but the terror lingered. What would happen to me if Roslyn was my mate? If I took things too far? She broke down all of my defenses with a simple shuddering cry of pleasure. How could I trust myself not to let the demon inside, who was desperate to see that same panic in her eyes, take over?

But just the thought of her writhing under me was enough to banish that fear. As I paced my room, working to control myself, I groaned. She was every-fucking-where. My gaze lit upon a flash of white underneath my desk.

I blurred over to it, the balled-up knickers dangling from one of my fingers.

"Well, well, well. You didn't just like it. You got off on it. You stayed and watched the whole bloody show, didn't you?"

I pressed the cotton against my nose and breathed deep. They were still damp. Soaked.

Christ.

She'd seen me, what I am, what I need, and she'd wanted it. Craved it as much as I.

The proof of it was too much for me.

How could I deny myself when she wanted it as badly as I did?

I couldn't.

I wouldn't.

Standing, I grabbed my trousers, then tugged them on.

"Careful what you wish for, petal. You just might get it. In fact . . . I think you shall."

CHAPTER
NINE
GAVIN

I followed her intoxicating scent, not to her room as I'd expected, but to the library.

She didn't hear me come in, and I took a second to study the fall of her hair over her shoulder, the delicate curve of her throat as she flipped through the pages of the book in her hand, the way she chewed on her lower lip. She was so fragile.

I wanted to break her and then put the pieces back together. Preferably with my lips and teeth and tongue . . . and cum.

"You dropped these," I muttered, tossing the knickers onto the floor at her feet.

Her cheeks went a delightful shade of rose. She opened and closed her mouth, clearly searching for some sort of explanation.

"Don't you dare lie to me, petal."

"I didn't say anything."

"You were working up to it."

She lifted her chin. "So what if I did leave them behind?"

"You know, it's considered rude to spy on people."

Narrowing her eyes, she set her jaw. Oh, she was playing at being defiant. I couldn't stop the smirk that twisted my lips.

"It's considered cheating to be with someone other than your wife."

"Did I fuck him?"

"N-no."

"Did he fuck me?"

"No . . . "

"Then how exactly did I cheat on you?"

"You were naked and—"

"And what, petal?"

"Aroused."

"And thinking of you."

Her breath left her in a whoosh.

"That's right. How does it make you feel, knowing as I did those things, I imagined I was doing them to you? That it was your back I whipped. Your submission I craved."

Her eyes went glassy, her flush deepening. Fucking hell, yes. I knew that look. She would be panting for me soon.

"You wanted it to be you, didn't you?"

Taking her lush bottom lip between her teeth, she flicked her gaze away, diverting her attention to the crackling fire in the hearth.

"Petal. Look at me." My voice was stern, commanding, and the need that slammed into me when she instantly obeyed had me damn near vibrating.

"Answer. Me."

"Y-yes, my lord."

She was perfect. And mine.

It was time I proved it to both of us.

"Take off your clothes."

48

"Pardon?"

"Do not make me repeat myself."

Her fingers trembled as she lifted her jumper over her head and then shimmied out of her skirt. While my petal was small, she was still gracefully curvaceous. A tiny waist, only emphasized by mouth watering teardrop-shaped breasts and hips that flared out in a soft swell. I'd wager if she turned around for me, her arse would be a perfect heart shape.

"What now?"

"Come here to me. And bring me those knickers of yours. You left them for me after all." She took a step, bending down to reach for the fabric. "No. On your knees. Hold them with your teeth and crawl."

Her eyes widened as my order registered. Her body gave her away. My words had her pressing her thighs together as she slowly sank down, holding my gaze the entire time. This was the first of many new things my innocent creature would do for me. I looked forward to introducing her to them all.

Her firsts belonged to me.

She was fucking exquisite as she moved across the floor. What could have looked silly was bloody sinful. She had an innate grace and newly discovered sexuality that made each roll of her shoulders primal. And the way her breasts swayed with each move she made had me wanting to bite those nipples and feed from her here and now.

I forgot how to breathe as I watched her. All I could hear was the rush of my blood in my ears. Could I simply pull her to her feet and free my aching cock here and now? All I had to do was lift her into my arms and spear her on my length.

She reached me then, rising to her knees and tilting her

head back, the cotton in her mouth an offering. I leaned down, taking her cheeks in my hand and squeezing until her mouth opened. Pulling the knickers free, I tucked them into the pocket of my trousers.

"Do you like how you taste, petal?"

She nodded, a little whimper escaping her.

"I wonder if you'll like how *I* taste as well." I sat in the leather chair behind me, opening my trousers and spreading my legs wide. Her tongue darted out, wetting her lips. I don't even think she realized she did it. "Do you want to taste me, petal? Do you want me to fuck that pretty mouth of yours until you're choking on my dick?"

She nodded.

"Say it."

"Yes."

"Yes, what?

"Yes, my lord."

Oh, the things she could do with three words.

"My title never sounded as good as it does from your lips, but I meant tell me what you want."

"I . . . I . . . whatever you desire."

I swallowed as all the blood in my body rushed to my weeping cock. She had no idea what she was asking for.

"We'll get to that. Right now, I am more interested in what *you* want me to do."

"Fu . . . put it in my mouth."

A dark chuckle escaped before I could school myself. "What was that?"

"Let me suck on your . . . manhood."

"Oh, petal. If you want my cock, you have to ask for it. My wife cannot be a simpering miss. Not when I want her to be my dirty little slut."

50

She sucked in a sharp breath and squirmed, her hands tightening at her sides.

"Are you my dirty little slut?"

She nodded, a little uncertain but so very aroused.

"Use your words, petal. Prove it."

"I want . . . I want your c-cock."

I took my shaft in my hand, slowly working my palm along its straining length. Her eyes followed the movement, her breath stuttering, her nipples sharp little points. I knew if I reached between her thighs, she'd be fucking dripping. My very own waterfall.

"Put your hands on me."

"Where?"

Reaching down, I took her by the wrist and placed her palm on my thigh. "Here."

"Gavin—"

"What was that?"

Her gaze flicked to meet mine. "My lord."

"Very good. Now suck my cock like you were born for it."

She lowered her head, and my fingers threaded in the silk mass of hair I'd been craving. I gripped the strands tight enough that she cried out, goosebumps erupting across her bare back. Fuck me, I could feel the soft whisper of her breath across my crown.

Her reaction to that first hint of pain was nearly my undoing. We'd barely begun her introduction, and she was already a natural. So responsive. So eager to please.

She licked me right as the door opened.

"What the hell is this?" Daniel's voice broke through the veil of this trial session with my Roslyn.

She tensed, her whole demeanor changing as I released my hold on her hair.

"I'm quite busy," I gritted out.

"Was I not satisfactory, my lord?"

"You'd dare question me?"

"You said she didn't matter. She wasn't enough. Just a business transaction."

I clenched my jaw, feeling Roslyn's eyes boring into me as she slipped away. I didn't meet her gaze, too furious at the interruption to deal with her tender feelings. "Get out," I snarled.

"Don't bother," she said, gathering her clothes and hastily putting them on. "I'm leaving."

She shoved past Daniel, rushing toward the stairs, her hair flying behind her like dark waves on a stormy sea.

Daniel dropped to his knees with a wicked smirk, beginning to crawl toward me. Guilt swarmed around me. I shouldn't have used him to work through my own struggles. "Get up," I commanded.

He did as he was told, but the incredulity in his eyes spoke volumes.

"Earlier was a mistake."

"My lord, I know you tried to break things off before the wedding, but . . . I had hoped you'd come to your senses. She doesn't understand you. She's not made for you like I am. Roslyn Blackthorne is a precious princess. She could never be what you need."

I stood, rage boiling at the surface. "Keep her name out of your mouth." Then I stared through him as though he'd never existed at all.

He gaped at me. "I-I'm sorry, my lord."

"We are through. To ensure you get the message this time, pack your things. I want you gone in the next hour."

"Gavin, please."

"Your insolence knows no bounds. Do not embarrass yourself further. Leave."

I couldn't bring myself to feel anything more than apathy at the sight of the tears shimmering in Daniel's gaze. I'd never had feelings for him, but clearly he'd developed them for me. I should have ended things sooner. It was my own fault for allowing the lines to be blurred. Sexual release and love were two different things in my world. I'd never loved anyone, and I'd made him no promises. He knew what he was getting when we entered our arrangement.

Roslyn, however . . .

She was my wife. The only one who'd make her cry was me. And those would be tears of pleasure.

It didn't matter what I'd said in the beginning. From the second she placed herself at my feet, everything had changed. And now, after a glimpse of what it could be like between us, I'd never let her go.

CHAPTER
TEN
ROSIE

You said she didn't matter. She wasn't enough. Just a business transaction.

Gavin's lover's words echoed in my mind as I ran from the room. Just a transaction. I'd been right; I was such a fool.

I'd known going into this that Gavin Donoghue wasn't a good man. But then I'd gone and started *wanting* things, and all that *want* clouded my mind. Made me forget just what kind of man I'd married. Cold. Callous. Unfeeling. He didn't let himself care about anyone. Least of all me.

It would have been so much easier to protect myself if he hadn't touched me. Hadn't given me a taste of what a genuine marriage could be like between us. But he did, and now I knew I couldn't be satisfied with anything else.

I wanted all of him or nothing at all.

A business transaction with sex thrown in the mix wouldn't end well for me. I'd fall in love with him, with a man I'd never really have, and then I'd go mad.

Every day my heart would break all over again.

It wasn't a life. It was a prison sentence.

Torture.

This is all your fault, Roslyn. You're the one who threw your-self under the bus. Who offered yourself up like a prize pig. When did you get so stupid? You're supposed to be the smart one.

I had to get out of here. I'd never survive him if I didn't. I'd go home, back to Blackthorne Manor, and pretend I hadn't already fallen a little in love with a man who'd never truly want me. And love aside, in one night, Gavin Donoghue unlocked more dark desires than I ever thought existed inside me. The need to be dominated, degraded, and praised. The hunger for pain and pleasure to be joined together. The twisted urge to watch him bring another man release.

I shuddered as a flood of need rushed between my thighs in response to those memories. Gavin's stiff length glistening at the tip as he stroked himself in front of the camera. His harsh breaths, the way he tensed as he made the other man cry out in pain.

Goodness, Roslyn, get it together.

I had to focus, not get lost in a state of arousal right here in the hall. *When had I gotten here? Where the devil am I?*

The castle was a labyrinth. I didn't even know which wing I was in. Nothing looked familiar. I spun in a circle, starting back the way I'd come when I heard this hiss of a conversation. I could only make out one word, but it was enough to stop me in my tracks.

Blackthornes.

They were talking about me. My family.

I crept closer to the door that was slightly ajar, my heart in my throat as the duke and duchess's voices grew louder.

"The blasted sun is rising. I don't want to go another night with her in this castle and us not able to walk in the day."

"Patience, darling. She's already given Gavin a taste. He'll handle her during daylight hours, and then we'll begin."

"If she doesn't give us what we want, we're fucked, Felicity. She'll simply be another burden to care for. We can't very well dispose of the Blackthorne princess without some kind of censure." The duke's rumbled words made me cringe.

"Oh, ye of little faith. Gavin will bring her to heel. You saw how the bitch was practically in heat as she stared at him with those puppy eyes of hers. She was begging him to love her. She'll give him his heir, and then we can use the baby to keep her in line, and if she . . . *dies in childbirth*, no one will be the wiser. We'll lock her away, siphon her blood slowly, and have our very own Blackthorne-Donoghue bloodline, and Gavin will be free of this albatross hanging around his neck."

"And what if she doesn't get with child right away?"

"Then we use that brother of hers. You saw how protective she was of him. If she doesn't want to obey, then we blackmail her into submission."

"Oh, my devious little duchess. I love it when you plot to destroy our enemies."

A soft moan filtered into the hall. The rustle of fabric. The unmistakable sound of a zipper. "And when she doesn't submit, we kill every. Last. Creature. She loves."

The deep, masculine groan in response had me shuddering. Bile rose in my throat, not only because they were discussing the murder of my entire family, but because they were quite literally getting off on the idea.

Vile. Depraved. *Evil*. That's what the Donoghues were. Absolute evil.

I couldn't stay here another second. I had to get out. Not just for myself, but to save my family.

I was already running through the hallway back toward the stairs when a terrible thought occurred to me.

I couldn't just run. So long as I was alive with ties to their son, they would come for my family and me. I'd never be free.

There was only one solution to this problem. Roslyn Blackthorne had to die.

CHAPTER
ELEVEN
GAVIN

"You bloody fool, what are you doing to yourself? Pacing like a tiger in a fucking cage over a woman you could have made yours time and time again last night."

I wasn't sure why I hadn't gone after her. Between her exit and dealing with Daniel, it just seemed best to let her ride out her tantrum and return to her once her emotions had cooled. But with every passing second, it became more difficult to make myself take those steps. I didn't want to face her. To face myself. To see the emotional wounds I'd inflicted. Somehow those weren't the same as physical marks. Her heart was off-limits. Her body, though? There was a completely different set of rules.

I hadn't even needed to look at her to know what a blow it had been hearing Daniel lob my words like a grenade. It haunted me, that moment. We'd been on the cusp of something, she and I, but any foundation we'd built had been destroyed by his jealousy.

I felt guilty, which made me angry. I hadn't done anything wrong. I had said those things, and in the moment, I'd meant them. She wasn't supposed to be mine in more than name. Our compatibility was a boon. An unexpected perk of the job.

For both of us.

She should feel lucky. Blessed by the realization. At my feet begging for attention.

Not off in her room sulking like a petulant brat.

This was not a love match. I'd given her my name, not my heart.

Love was never on the table. She needed to be reminded of that.

So I'd remind her right bloody now.

She'd had enough time to stew. I was finished with this behavior. It was time for me to make my wife understand exactly what being married to me would be.

The promise of sated lust and her cries sang through my blood, humming inside me and thickening my cock as I thought of all the ways I'd make her see reason. I stormed out of my room and straight to hers, where I threw open the door without warning. I expected to find her curled on her bed, tear tracks marring her perfect skin. But she wasn't there. The room was empty.

No trace remained save the lingering scent of her. Panic and disappointment warred for top billing in my head. Why wasn't she here, ready to get on her knees and beg me to be the master of her body?

A growl of frustration rumbled in my chest, my knuckles going white and the wood groaning beneath my tight grasp.

Where are you, petal?

Instinct, like a tiny annoying buzz in my ear, had me turning to look at her armoire. The door was barely cracked, but it was a damning bit of evidence. Peering inside, anger burned in my gut. No clothes. No luggage. Nothing. I turned on my heel, my gaze sweeping the room and stopping on the piece of paper in the center of her perfectly made bed.

My Lord,

I'm sorry I had to leave so quickly and without saying goodbye. As you know, my brother's mate has gone missing, and my family needs me. I hadn't intended on this visit being anything more than wedding planning. I certainly hadn't expected we'd be married within hours of my arrival. I didn't prepare for an extended stay or, frankly, anything that happened since I set foot in this house.

I was not prepared for you, my lord.

I find myself quite conflicted over everything that has transpired between us. I crave you in a way I don't understand, and that frightens me. But even more so, it has taught me a great deal about myself and my desires.

My family needs my help to show we are a united front as the attacks on my brother and his mate continue, and I cannot in good conscience hide away here with you.

Once Sunday is found, I will return to you. I'm asking for you to give me this time.

Time to make peace with my feelings. Time to say goodbye to my family. Time to ready myself for all that it means to be yours.

I know neither of us thought this would be more than a marriage of convenience. A way to settle the debt my family owes yours. I think, perhaps, it could end up being quite a bit more. I just . . . need a little time to wrap my head around it. To come to you able to offer complete submission.

Seeing you with him woke something inside me, something that gathered strength in the library. A creature of darkness hungry for pain at only your hand. But I can't give in to those desires until I understand them. Until I've had space from the wild storm you stir in my blood.

When I return, it will be to give myself to you.

Yours, Petal

I NEARLY CRUMPLED the letter as I let her words sink in. She needed space.

Space.

From.

Me.

She was topping me from the bottom already. I should go after her, bring her back and make her obey. Show her the room and all its toys. Give her something more she could remember whenever she caught a glance of her bare skin in the mirror and saw my lash marks on her back.

But then I read her missive again, tracing my fingers over the delicate script of her carefully written note. She intentionally used the nickname I'd given her. Called me her lord. Told me she wanted to be mine in the ways that I most desired.

She would come back.

I had to trust her to return. I had to relinquish control over this until she gave it all to me.

I was not a patient man, but I would give her this.

Because when my wife returned, I was going to ensure she never forgot who she belonged to.

Ten nights later

My mother's scream tore through the house.

"No! That little bitch ruined everything!"

Alarm bells clanged in my head, apprehension on their heels. I ran through the castle, desperate to see what had happened, because the sinking feeling in my bones said my petal was the cause.

What had she done now?

Any number of things could have happened, chief among them something that would ruin her blood and taint her usefulness to us. Tearing down the stairs, I found Mother and my father in the foyer, a missive in her hand.

"Mother? What is it? What's wrong?"

She spun around, her entire body trembling with rage.

"Your wife managed to cheat us after all."

"What do you mean?"

She laughed, but there was no humor in it, only hysteria. "She went and got herself killed. And we are left with nothing. No alliance. No heir. No blood of the sun. Nothing but another slight against us by those slippery snakes, the Blackthornes. And now you have to pretend to mourn her. My son, the widower."

I sat down hard on the stairs, my blood roaring in my ears. My mother continued to rant, but I was still caught on the first part.

Killed.

My wife ... my petal ... was dead.

She'd been promised to me in the night. But now she was lost.

Taken before I ever got to make her mine.

The story continues in Deal with the Demon, The Mate Games: Pestilence *Book 1.*
Keep reading for a sneak peek . . .

CHAPTER
TWELVE
ROSIE

"Fake your own death, Roslyn. Save your family. Go on the run. It'll be fine," I grumbled as I trudged through the cold, muddy Alaskan terrain, heading toward my goal. Asher Henry, hacker extraordinaire.

I snorted. "Extraordinaire, my tight rear end. I found you in less than a day."

My whole body was frozen, teeth chattering, exhaustion weighing me down. If I didn't get to his forking house soon, I'd actually die—nothing fake about it.

A pang went through my heart at the romanticized version of Gavin I held onto. Him finding my note, hoping I'd be true to my word and return to him. It must've worked, or the vampire would have come and stolen me away, back to the Donoghue castle. He had to know I was dead now too. Good.

The sight of a house at the crest of the hill had me picking up my pace. Almost there. I stepped on a root as I continued, the uneven ground sending me tumbling into the mixture of slushy snow and mud. But I was nearly to my goal. Asher would help me. He'd make sure Roslyn

PROMISED TO THE NIGHT

Blackthorne never appeared again. Give me a new name. A new life.

I reached his front door and weakly knocked, a bone-deep shiver clattering my teeth together. No answer. No lights. No sign of him.

"I'll just wait here, then," I mumbled. "You have to come home sometime."

I lost track of the hours as I sat on his porch, curled in on myself to try and stave off the worst of the wind. I may not be a human, but I wouldn't survive out in the elements like this for long. I'd already lost feeling in my fingers by the time wheels finally crunched through the snow. It was enough to make my heart stutter.

A door opened, and a deadly voice growled, "Don't fucking move."

I'd recognize that voice anywhere.

I unfurled myself, my gaze traveling up the bundled form of my would-be assailant, gun raised and trained on me.

Asher Henry, my black-hatted knight in technological armor. He didn't know it yet, but he was about to become my hero.

If I could convince him not to kill me first.

～

GRAB YOUR COPY OF *DEAL WITH THE DEMON*, *THE MATE GAMES: PESTILENCE BOOK 1* NOW!
KEEP READING FOR A SNEAK PEEK.

SNEAK PEEK: DEAL WITH THE DEMON

ASHER

Aurora Springs, Alaska

That witch was going to be the death of me after all. A hiss escaped me as a burn shot through the mark she'd saddled me with years ago. A parting gift for my unfortunate misstep.

I checked the spot on the back of my hand; just a small star right in the center. What the fuck? Was the thing growing? Instead of a single star, there was now a small cluster. Dread curled in my gut. What did this mean? How could I stop it? Whatever it was, it couldn't be good.

A loud crash from behind me pulled me out of my spiral of doom. Two wolf shifters and a burly lumberjack were locked in a scuffle. I had to get the hell out of here before this turned into a full-on bar brawl.

I pulled my collar up higher as I left the Tipsy Moose behind. I hadn't even been able to enjoy my beer before those fucking Mercer twins started a fight. They had thirty other days to act like a bunch of assholes, and they chose the one night a month where I came into town for my supply run. It was my only chance to stop in for a taste of semi-normal existence, and it had been ruined by dick-swinging shifters.

Fucking typical.

The wind kicked up, sending the curly hair of my fake beard fluttering across the hollow of my throat and tickling me without mercy. Maybe one day I wouldn't have to hide my identity, but as of right now, I was still the supernatural world's most wanted hacker. That meant a life of anonymous sex, zero meaningful relationships, and way too much wig adhesive. It was all fake names, deep cover, and high security for me. Unless I wanted to get caught and become the captive of that vengeful witch.

Hard pass. She'd already done enough damage.

I scratched at my chin with an annoyed grunt, my irritation rising when I felt the adhesive give way. Great. My goatee probably looked drunker than I did—than I was *supposed* to be.

The whole thing was bullshit, my night wrecked, and now I didn't even have a good buzz to make any of the effort worth it. I should have just waited until I got home. Then I could have cracked open one of the bottles of Jack I'd bought and found oblivion in the best way I knew. Alone.

I hated the need for these disguises, but it was the only way to maintain any sort of social life when, as far as the people of Aurora Springs knew, Asher Henry didn't exist. And I needed to keep it that way if I wanted to stay alive. In a town of one hundred and seventy-three people, that was a special sort of hell.

Thus I became Joe Baker, resident hermit and curmudgeonly fisherman. No one bothered me. No one cared if I ever showed my face.

Well, almost no one.

Starting up my old beater of a truck, I waited for the heat to blast and fill the cab. Even in the spring, it was cold here. But going into hiding meant isolation in a small, nowhere town. What better place than the near wilds of Alaska?

I drove the forty minutes up the winding path to my mountain fortress, mostly muttering to myself and ignoring the sorry excuse for music playing on the radio. It was really just a bunch of static with a random guitar strum here and there, but what could you expect from a town with one fucking station?

If the night had gone according to plan, I would have slept it off at Joe Baker's houseboat or any of the other properties I owned under various names. But since tonight had shit the bed before it even started, all I wanted was to go home. That meant my log cabin in the woods. The one filled with technology so advanced not even the military had access to most of it, and no one in Aurora Springs, let alone anywhere else, would find it on any kind of map. Google Earth could fuck right off.

As I pulled past the camouflaged gate hiding my property from the prying eyes of wayward hikers, I frowned. The beams of my headlights flashed across strange tracks in the muddy earth of the dirt road.

"What the fuck?"

My pulse raced, adrenaline spiking as the path continued toward my house. Animal? Maybe. I'd encountered my share of wildlife here. They were the only creatures who breached my walls.

But as soon as I parked, I saw the culprit. A dirty lump

huddled against my door. Stringy dark hair hanging in front of their—no, *her*—face.

Reaching under the seat of my truck, I pulled the revolver I kept hidden there out of its holster. You never knew what you'd come up against out here. I'd learned that the hard way.

I got out, breath tight as I raised the gun and switched off the safety. Then I cocked the hammer and said, "Don't fucking move."

Her head snapped up, and she pinned me with eyes the color of burnished gold. My heart stuttered. I knew those eyes. That face. I'd stared at them far too many times from the glow of my computer screens under the guise of "research." But she wasn't my assignment, shouldn't have been on my fucking radar at all. And yet I hadn't been able to look away even after—

"You're dead."

Her stats flashed in my memory:

ROSLYN "ROSIE" BLACKTHORNE

AGE: 21

SPECIES: VAMPIRE-HUMAN HYBRID

(NEVER TURNED)

PARENTS: CASHEL AND OLIVIA BLACKTHORNE

SIBLINGS: NOAH AND WESTLEY BLACKTHORNE

STATUS: DECEASED

CAUSE OF DEATH: HOUSE FIRE

"Not dead enough, it would seem." She got to wobbly feet, her eyes tired, face dirt-streaked and pale. "Asher, I need your help."

"Why the fuck should I help you? How did you even find me?"

A proud, exhausted smile flitted across her face. "You're not the only one with a certain skill set."

The knowledge that I'd been hacked sent a bolt of terror straight through me. If she'd been able to find me, who else could? I'd be so damn careful. There weren't any bread-crumbs, cyber or otherwise. I was as off the map as possi-ble. Yet her presence here, the fact that she'd called me by my name, proved just how fucking wrong I was. *Christ, I was going to need to do a full security sweep.*

"Then why do you need me at all?"

"Could you put that thing down?"

I glanced at the gun I still had aimed between her eyes. "Shit. Sorry."

"And I need you because you have connections I don't."

"Such as?"

"People, papers, access to new documents."

"So you're on the run."

"Well, I can't exactly go around as the late Roslyn Black-thorne, now can I?"

"That's what this is about? You want a new identity?"

"I need to make sure Rosie stays dead and buried. God knows I went to enough effort killing her. No one can know I'm alive. Not even my family."

"What are you running from?"

Her expression went grave. "My husband."

GRAB YOUR COPY OF DEAL WITH THE DEMON, THE MATE GAMES: PESTILENCE BOOK 1 TO KEEP READING!

THE MATE GAMES UNIVERSE
BY K. LORAINE & MEG ANNE

Also by Meg Anne

The Keepers

A Guardian/Ward High Fantasy Romance

The Dreamer (A Keeper's Prequel)

The Keepers Legacy

The Keepers Retribution

The Keepers Vow

The Keepers Boxset

The Forsaken

A Rejected Mates/Enemies-To-Lovers Romantasy

Prisoner of Steel & Shadow

Queen of Whispers & Mist

Court of Death & Dreams

Prince of Sea & Stars

A Standalone MMF Romantasy Adventure

Gypsy's Curse

A Psychic/Detective Star-Crossed Lovers UF Romance

Visions Of Death

Visions Of Vengeance

Visions Of Triumph

The Gypsy's Curse: The Complete Collection

Also by K. Loraine

~

STANDALONES

CURSED (MFM SLEEPING BEAUTY RETELLING)

~

REVERSE HAREM STANDALONES

THEIR VAMPIRE PRINCESS (A REVERSE HAREM ROMANCE)

ALL THE QUEEN'S MEN (A FAE REVERSE HAREM ROMANCE)

ABOUT MEG ANNE

USA Today and international bestselling paranormal and fantasy romance author Meg Anne has always had stories running on a loop in her head. They started off as daydreams about how the evil queen (aka Mom) had her slaving away doing chores, and more recently shifted into creating backgrounds about the people stuck beside her during rush hour. The stories have always been there; they were just waiting for her to tell them.

Like any true SoCal native, Meg enjoys staying inside curled up with a good book and her fur babies . . . or maybe that's just her. You can convince Meg to buy just about anything if it's covered in glitter or rhinestones, or make her laugh by sharing your favorite bad joke. She also accepts bribes in the form of baked goods and Mexican food.

Meg is best known for her leading men #MenbyMeg, her inevitable cliffhangers, and making her readers laugh out loud, all of which started with the bestselling Chosen series.

ABOUT K. LORAINE

USA Today Bestselling author Kim Loraine writes steamy contemporary and sexy paranormal romance. **You'll find her paranormal romances written under the name K. Loraine and her contemporaries as Kim Loraine.** Don't worry, you'll get the same level of swoon-worthy heroes, sassy heroines, and an eventual HEA.

When not writing, she's busy herding cats (raising kids), trying to keep her house sort of clean, and dreaming up ways for fictional couples to meet.